STRANGE SCOUT TALES!

BOOK TWO: THE LOCH NESS LOCK-IN

MATTHEW CODY

ART BY STEVE LAMBE

RODALE
KiDS

Text copyright © 2018 by Matthew Cody
Cover art and interior illustrations copyright © 2018 by Steve Lambe

All rights reserved. Published in the United States by Rodale Kids, an imprint of Random House Children's Books, a division of Penguin Random House LLC, New York.

Rodale and the colophon are registered trademarks and Rodale Kids is a trademark of Penguin Random House LLC.

Visit us on the Web! rhcbooks.com

Educators and librarians, for a variety of teaching tools, visit us at RHTeachersLibrarians.com

Library of Congress Cataloging-in-Publication Data is available upon request.
ISBN 978-1-63565-060-0 (trade) — ISBN 978-1-63565-045-7 (ebook)

Printed in the United States of America
10 9 8 7 6 5 4 3 2 1
First Edition

CONTENTS

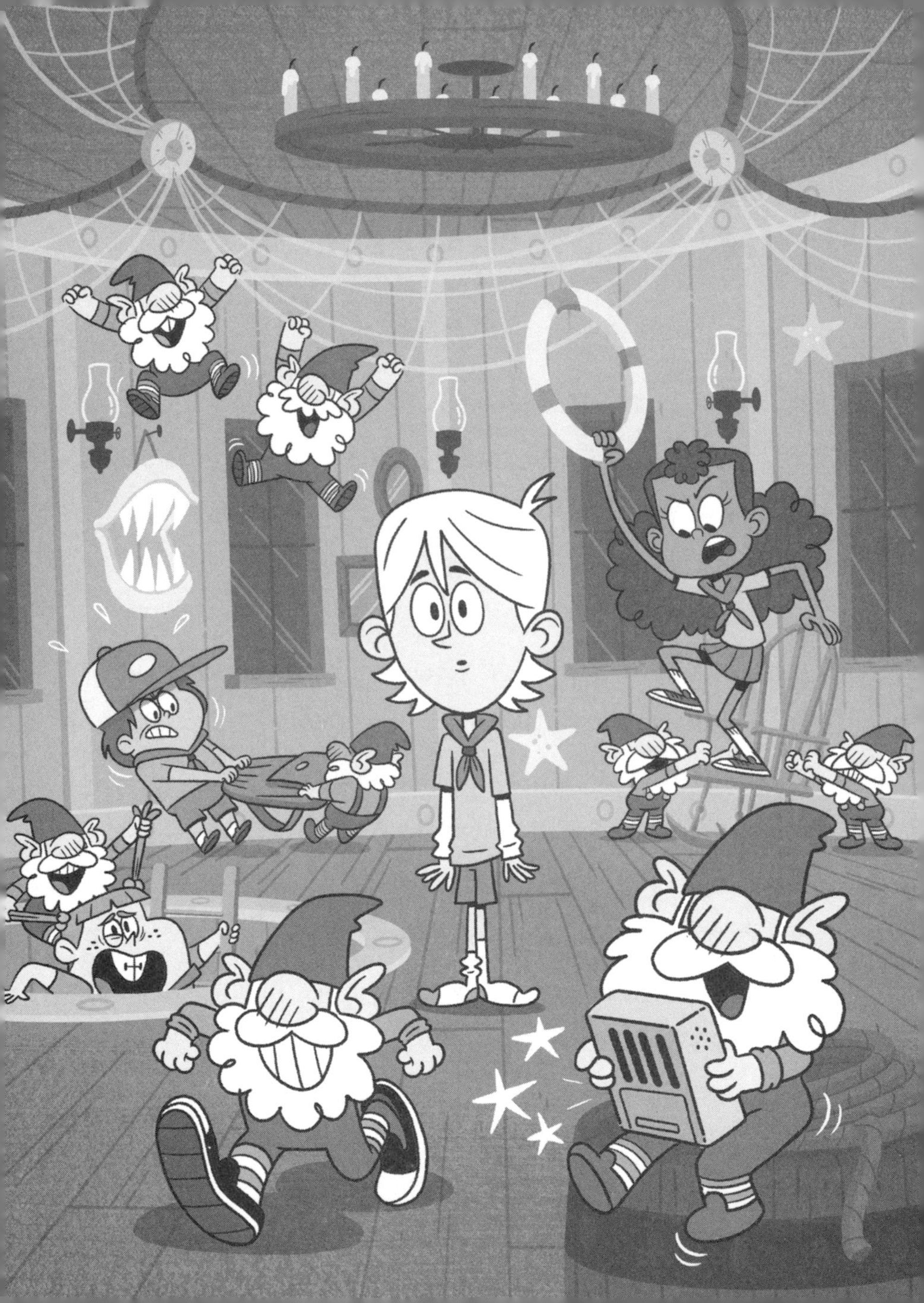

IN DEEP WATER

This is not as bad as it looks.

Okay, it's almost as bad, but there is one tiny silver lining that you may not pick up on right away— I'm wearing my very best socks. On any other day that a red cap decided to steal my boots, I'd be chasing after him in dirty socks with holes in the toes.

But on this day, I had my clean socks on.

What are red caps, you ask? Well, as an example I'll point out that little beastie wearing my boots. Just know this—red caps are a pain.

And who am I? Ben Beederman's the name. Sorry, I figured you might've already read volume one of my magnum opus *Strange Scout Tales: How to Merit in Monsters*. But if you haven't read it yet, don't worry—I'll try to fill you in as we go.

Anyway, back to red caps. To understand those little beasties, you'll need to understand what it means to be a Strange Scout. No, I don't mean like *weirdo* strange, I mean like unique, mysterious, and, yes, sometimes monstrous. But only in the very best sense of the word!

Because to be a Strange Scout is to believe this one important truth—monsters are cool! (Okay, red caps may be the exception.)

When my parents sent me off to Camp Spirit, they thought I'd be learning about nature and honor and all that traditional scout stuff—which I did. But they didn't know I'd also be recruited into a top-secret branch of the scouts called the Strange Scouts. See, the Strange Scouts have been around since the days of President Teddy Roosevelt, and for all that time they've been protecting one of the earth's most valuable natural wonders: monsters. This old guy, Walter, is my Scout Master, and those other yahoos in the picture with me—Ginger, Asma, and

Manuel—are my troop mates and my best friends.

We are Troop D . . . *D* for *danger*!

What? *D* for *dweeb*? Wait a minute, you *did* read the first book, didn't you?!

Whatever.

The point is that we went to this lame-sounding camp and saved a Bigfoot named Eugene from drinking from a poisoned water supply, and so we became awesome Strange Scouts and we can call ourselves Troop Danger now if we want to. So there.

Whew. Really, none of that has anything to do with the story I need to tell you, of which those red caps are only one part. It's really a story about a haunted lighthouse on the shore of Scotland's Loch Ness, super gross Scottish food, and yes . . . the Loch Ness Monster! It was the adventure of a lifetime in a faraway land where our powers of teamwork and resourcefulness were put to the test!

Of course, we're Troop D, which means it went about as well as you'd expect. So, let's back up a bit before we get to the red caps, Scotland, and Loch Ness.

Because this story begins with a field trip.

2

WET BEHIND THE EARS

Earning our Teamwork Badges was supposed to be a—what do you call it?—a *formality*. See, Walter had planned this big overseas trip to Scotland for us to see the famous Loch Ness. Did you know that a "loch" is just what they call a lake in Scotland? Cool, right? I'm actually hoping it'll catch on everywhere.

It may not be exactly common for scouts to travel overseas, but the Strange Scouts are anything but common. And Walter insisted that seeing Loch Ness was an important

step in understanding what it was
to be a Strange Scout. In many ways,
Loch Ness represented what the
scouts were all about. Here was a
mysterious place, shrouded in legend,
protecting what might very well
be the oldest living monster in the
world—the Loch Ness Monster!

It was a trip meant to educate us
and instill a sense of wonder about the
hidden world of nature.

Yeah, whatever. I was all about the haggis.

Have you heard of haggis? Google it. I'll wait.

See? How many opportunities do you get in life to actually dare your friends to eat a sheep's stomach stuffed with . . . stuff? It's seriously all I thought about for weeks before the trip. I literally dreamed about it.

So the plan was:

1. Go to Scotland and find a
   haggis.
2. Dare one of my friends to
   eat the haggis.
3. Be crowned the coolest kid
   who ever lived.

Foolproof, right?

I was so ready for this trip. On to
Scotland!

3

A WET BIRD NEVER FLIES AT NIGHT

Our parents all knew we were going to Scotland to see Loch Ness, but when we told them about the trip we conveniently left out the whole "monster" thing. Part of the mission of the Strange Scouts is to protect these monsters, and keeping them secret is important. When I met everyone at the airport, I was happy to see that the other members of Troop D hadn't changed much since the last time we were together.

Asma had packed an entire suitcase full of travel-size bottles of hand sanitizer, Manuel had packed a suitcase full of video games, and Ginger . . . well, Ginger had trouble packing her suitcase at all because

she'd lost her temper and stomped
on it until it was all bent out of shape.

Everyone's parents came to the
airport to see us off, and that meant
some teary goodbyes. Me, I was totally
focused on the mission.

After we'd said our goodbyes,
Walter called us over to have a Troop D
huddle. "All righty then, scouts. Time
for your mission briefing," he said. "So,
Ben and Manuel, turn off those darned

newfangled higgamabobs and pay
attention!"

Walter, by the way, was one of the
first Strange Scouts ever—he actually
received a badge from Teddy Roosevelt
himself—so that makes him roughly
a hundred billion years old. To Walter,
anything invented after the 1940s is
a higgamabob or a whatsajabbit or a
kewkathangle.

"Now, this trip isn't going to be all safe
and cozy like Camp Spirit," Walter said.
"This is gonna be real scouts business!"

I could have reminded Walter that at camp we had been menaced by a Bigfoot with indigestion—hardly a safe and cozy experience. But I caught Asma giving me that "Keep your trap shut for once" look and stayed quiet.

Walter continued, "Now, you four are a handful for an old fella like me to look after all by myself, so I invited a chaperone along for the trip."

No. He wouldn't. Why would he?

"Scouts, you all remember Scout Master Spitzer?"

Apparently, he would.

Spitzer was the Scout Master who made our lives miserable back at Camp Spirit, and we still ended up saving him from getting accidentally squashed by Eugene the Bigfoot. The guy was a

total bully, and he hated the Strange
Scouts even though he had been one
when he was a kid.

I couldn't think of any reason
Walter would invite him along except
that there wasn't anyone else who
even knew the Strange Scouts existed.
I guess Spitzer was all Walter had.

Spitzer grinned at us. It wasn't friendly. "The only reason I agreed to come along on this trip is because Scotland has the best golfing in the world, and I'm working on my game. So, three ground rules before we get going: One, I'm in charge. Two, I'm in charge. And three, you're *not* in charge. Anyone who forgets these rules will be cleaning the latrines!"

Asma raised her hand. "Uh, sir? We're going to Scotland, not camp. There won't be latrines."

Spitzer's grin grew even wider. "Oh, I'm sure we can find a toilet or two that needs scrubbing over there. Call it a scout public service."

Asma, who's a germophobe *and* a hypochondriac, looked ready to faint.

"Now, now," said Walter. "No need

for all that. I'm sure we're all going to
get along just fine. So let's get a move
on. We've got a plane to catch."

But the thing was, Walter started
off in the opposite direction, away from
the terminal.

"Walter, aren't we going the wrong
way?" I asked as we hurried to catch up.
"All the departing flights are back there."

"Strange Scouts don't fly first class,"
grumbled Walter. "And I'm not sitting for
five hours next to a screaming baby with

nothing but a bag of peanuts to distract me. We're taking the *Green Goose*!"

Spitzer stopped in his tracks. "Really, Walter? You think that's a good idea?"

But either Walter didn't hear him or he ignored him, because the old guy disappeared behind a door marked TERMINAL D: PRIVATE AIRCRAFT ONLY.

"Wow," said Manuel. "Does that mean the Strange Scouts have their own private jet?"

Spitzer lost all the color in his face. "The *Green Goose* isn't a jet. Heck, it's barely a plane. I hope you kids brought your barf bags."

He took a deep breath and followed Walter through the door, and we were left wondering what we'd gotten ourselves into.

Again.

STILL WATERS RUN DEEP

Here's a funny thing: I learned that night that I do not get airsick.

Too bad the same can't be said for the rest of my friends.

I wouldn't exactly call Walter an ace pilot, but he got us to Scotland in one piece. After Spitzer took a

few minutes to kiss solid ground, we rented an old bus and drove to Loch Ness. Along the way, Walter pointed out crumbling old castles next to endless fields of what looked like tall propellers stuck into the ground.

"What're those?" I asked.

"Those are wind farms!" answered Asma. "I read about them. All those wind turbines are generating electricity using wind power."

"Yep," said Walter. "Scotland's a fascinating mix of the ancient and the newfangled. Of course, their greatest national treasure is Nessie, the monster of Loch Ness."

"You all can keep your moldy old castles and wind farms," said Spitzer. "As soon as we find a golf course, I'm hitting the first tee."

"Visiting Nessie is a tradition that's
as old as the Strange Scouts themselves,"
said Walter. "It's a great honor to meet
her, and not every scout gets the chance.
See, she's not only the oldest known
monster in the world, she's also the
shyest. For such an enormous creature,
it's amazing that she can pass by
without leaving a trace. . . ."

But Walter's words trailed off as
we drove within sight of the lakeshore.
A wind farm lay in ruins nearby, with

turbines snapped in half and some
smashed flat. And from the weird
tracks in the mud, it looked like
whatever had destroyed them had
come out of the lake itself!

Walter stopped the bus, and we all
got out to take a look. A local constable
was already on the scene, taking a
statement from some rich-looking guy
in a business suit jacket and a kilt.

"Only caught a glimpse of the
creature as it was slithering back into
the water," the businessman was saying.
"But no doubt it was her. The Loch

Ness Monster tore up the wind farm!"

"Phooey!" said Walter as he stomped over to him. "Since when has Nessie destroyed anything?"

The constable and the businessman looked Walter up and down. I have to say, an old guy in a scout uniform shouting in your face probably doesn't make the best first impression.

"Who are you?" the businessman asked.

"Scout Master Walter Simmons. Who are *you*?"

"Martin MacGregor," answered the man. "I own MacGregor's Classic Golf Green."

"Wait a minute!" said Spitzer, pushing his way in front of Walter. "You mean *the* MacGregor's Classic? I've

been dying to golf there for years!"

MacGregor grinned. "Well, the wait's over, laddie. It's over yonder. We're expanding, too! Just broke new ground today at the construction site. Soon it'll be double the size!"

He pointed to a nearby collection of lights and towers. On the drive in, I'd thought it was some kind of crazy mall, but now that I looked closer I spotted fake castles, windmills, and what looked like a giant plastic lake monster. Kids were trying to hit a golf ball into the monster's mouth, and when one of them succeeded, the plastic monster breathed smoke.

"Hold on, Spitzer!" said Ginger. "Are you telling us that you came all this way to play *Putt-Putt* golf?"

Spitzer's cheeks turned red as he glowered down at the tiny girl. "It's called *miniature* golf, and it's a perfectly respectable sport," he said.

Ginger didn't flinch under Spitzer's glare. She did snort, though, as she struggled not to laugh in the Scout Master's face.

"All right, enough," said Walter.

"Let's get back to the topic at hand."

But MacGregor turned his back on us and said, "The topic is done. I know what I saw—Nessie's gone berserk, and no piece of property along the Loch Ness shoreline is safe anymore! I thought those wind farms were an eyesore before, but now look at 'em. If you know what's good for you, you'll all steer clear of the lake until this problem's dealt with."

Then MacGregor stomped off to his mini-golf course, leaving us alone with the constable.

"Constable," said Walter. "You can't believe—"

But the constable held up his hands. "People have been claiming to have seen old Nessie for hundreds of years, but no one's ever heard of her doing harm. Heck, my granddad used to tell his teacher that Nessie ate his homework! But MacGregor's a respected man around here, and this property damage has to be taken seriously. We'll look into it. In the meantime, I think tourists should use caution. Stay out of the water!"

WATER YOU GONNA DO ABOUT IT?

Walter was awfully quiet when we got back on the bus, while Spitzer talked our ears off about his favorite mini-golf courses all around the world. He even showed us pictures of his trophy case back home, which was filled with those cheap plastic toys you can earn as prizes.

Now, back at Camp Spirit, Troop D had been forced to sleep in ramshackle old cabins that leaked when it rained and creaked when the wind blew, but nothing could have prepared us for our "accommodations" at Loch Ness.

The sun had gone down by the time we stopped for the night. I'd expected a cheap hotel. Maybe a run-down cottage. What we got instead was a creepy old lighthouse straight out of a scary movie. Asma, Ginger, and I couldn't believe our eyes. Manuel wouldn't have, either, if he'd ever bothered to look up from his video game. To tell you the truth, I'm not sure if he even knew we'd made it to Scotland yet.

"Welcome to the Strange Scouts Chapter House, Scotland Division," said Walter.

"It looks kinda dirty," said Asma.

"Hogwash!" answered Walter. "Every scout that's ever been through our ranks has spent the night in this here lighthouse."

Asma shook her head. "Did any of them bother to clean it? You know household dust is a serious allergen."

"Shouldn't we maybe stay someplace where we can get some dinner?" I asked.

I actually wasn't hungry at all, but I hadn't forgotten the haggis, either. I could just picture it: We'd all sit down to dinner, I'd order the biggest haggis on the menu for the whole table, and then I'd make sure to get a picture of their faces when it arrived.

Then I'd have that picture put on a T-shirt.

And posters.

And I'd make it my screen saver.

"You've all got your camping provisions," said Walter. "So you won't go hungry. And you'll all have a nice quiet night's rest once you take care of the red cap."

"Huh?" said Ginger. "What's a red cap?"

"I believe Ben has the scouts' handbook," said Walter. "Page 180, if I remember correctly."

My handbook, or *The Strange Scouts Handbook of Cryptozoology and Manners,* as it was properly called, was part scout guide and part monster encyclopedia. Also, it was a smelly old relic that gathered dust and grew mold in equal measure. But it was filled with all sorts of valuable information on knot tying, camping, and monsters— the usual Strange Scouts stuff.

I flipped to the correct page. "It says here that red caps are small, gnomish creatures that make their homes in old castles and lighthouses— places so decrepit that they've been abandoned by humans."

Ginger glanced up at the ancient lighthouse. "Fits the bill."

I kept reading. "The red cap gets its name from its distinctive choice of headwear. . . ."

"Sounds cute," said Asma.

But I wasn't done. "However, the legend that their caps are red because they dip them in their enemies' blood is almost certainly without merit."

"Okay, I take it back," said Asma. "Definitely not cute."

LiGhThOuSe OvEr TrOuBlEd WaTeRs

"**Y**ou're not going to make us spend the night in there with one of those creatures, are you?" I asked.

The old Scout Master shrugged.
"The locals say this lighthouse is haunted, but it's really just the red cap

up to his usual mischief. Keep your wits about you, stay calm, and you'll be fine. The book says the whole bloody cap thing is a legend without merit, right?"

"*Almost* without merit," said Ginger. "Pretty important distinction!"

But Walter waved her worries away. "Follow the handbook's suggestions for handling a red cap and there'll be no problem. This is your first Strange Scouts lock-in!"

"And what will you be doing while we wrangle this red cap?" I asked.

Walter gazed out over the misty lake. "I gotta find out what all this Nessie business is about. But I'll be back to fetch you in the morning. Meanwhile, Scout Master Spitzer will keep an eye on the lighthouse from out here in the bus."

"Why can't Spitzer come inside with us?" asked Ginger.

"Whoa, that nasty little guy is *your* problem," answered Spitzer.

Walter shoved a shiny silver whistle into Ginger's hand. "Here. If you all think you're in over your heads, blow this and Spitzer will come get you out. Won't you, Spitzer?"

The thick-necked Scout Master sighed. "I guess."

"There," said Walter. "Now I got some investigating to do, so I'll see you all at sunup."

And with that, Scout Master Walter trudged off along the shore, disappearing into the mist.

As the rest of Troop D grabbed their sleeping bags out of the bus, I approached Spitzer. "Uh, excuse me, sir?"

He eyed me warily. "What is it, Beederman?"

"Well, Walter said that you were once a Strange Scout yourself, maybe one of the best." Actually, he'd said Spitzer was *the* best. My handbook had even belonged to him once upon a time. He'd written all sorts of useful

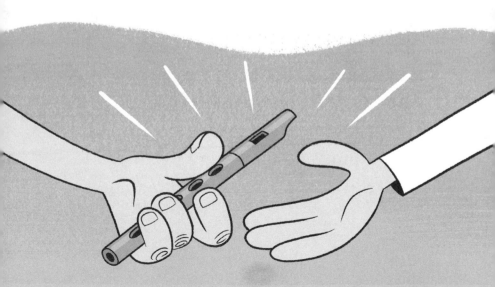

tips in the margins back when he was a kid. But for whatever reason, he practically loathed the Strange Scouts now.

"What's your point?" he asked, scowling.

"I was wondering if you ever did this. Walter said that every scout spent the night in that lighthouse, so I thought you might have some tips."

Spitzer leaned in close and said, "Yeah, I got a tip: Forget about all of this. You kids don't have what it takes, and if you know what's good for you, you'll quit while you still can."

Have I mentioned that Spitzer is also a bully? I mean, here's Exhibit A. All I did was ask for a bit of advice!

But I was not about to let him spook me now.

"Fine, don't help us," I said, getting angrier with every word. Seriously, I was channeling my inner Ginger. "We'll be just fine on our own!"

Spitzer laughed in my face. "You'll

be blowing that whistle ten minutes in. Just watch!"

And with that encouraging pep talk out of the way, Troop D marched up the steps to the lighthouse. I had the handbook and a newfound determination to prove Spitzer wrong. I was ready for anything.

Or so I thought.

7

LAKE FISHES OUT OF WATER

It was dark and spooky inside, just like you'd expect a haunted lighthouse to be. When the front door squeaked open on its rusty hinges, the sound echoed all the way to the signal room at the very top. Cobwebs crisscrossed the ceiling, and someone had stacked a few old tables and chairs against one wall. Several were missing legs. A few small windows set high in the wall let in a bit of moonlight.

"No light switch," said Ginger.

"Worse, no Wi-Fi," said Manuel.

We set up battery-powered camping lanterns and spread out our sleeping bags on the ground floor. So far, there was no sign of the red cap, but inside a dusty cupboard we did find a bunch of old butterfly nets and a few mason jars with holes poked in the lids.

"These might be useful," suggested

Asma. "What does the book say, Ben?"

"It's weird," I said, skimming the page on red caps. "It says that they are usually solitary creatures, but they have a unique defense mechanism: multiplication."

Ginger wrinkled her nose. "Multiplication? They do math at you?"

"It just says 'multiplication.' Weird. Oh, and it also warns that red caps are empaths."

"Emp-whats?" asked Ginger.

"Empaths. It means they can sense emotions. Says in here they like the calm quiet of abandoned places, but strong emotions such as fear, anxiety, and especially anger get them riled up."

Asma cleared her throat to get our

attention. "Um, I think we've got a visitor."

Standing on the table was a tiny creature wearing a red cap. He was calmly watching us, as if he'd been there the whole time. He blinked up at us with big, kitten-like eyes.

"Aww!" said Asma.

Then he picked his nose and flung it at her.

"Eww!"

The red cap mimicked her "eww" in his squeaky little voice, then grabbed his belly and laughed.

"All right," snapped Asma. "You don't have to be rude!"

The red cap blew a raspberry.

"Jeez," said Ginger. "Does the book say anything about red caps being beasties?"

"It doesn't matter," said Manuel. "This little guy's no threat. All we gotta do is keep our cool until sunrise and we'll have no prob—"

Manuel was cut off by a loud beep coming from his video game. "Whoops. Battery's almost dead. Anyone see an outlet where I can plug in?"

Asma, Ginger, and I shared worried looks. The three of us were thinking the exact same thing, which hadn't yet dawned on Manuel.

There was no electricity in the lighthouse, which meant no outlets.

Which meant Manuel was about to seriously freak out in three . . . two . . . one . . .

"Gah!" he screamed. "I'm gonna lose my progress! I'm too close to the save point now to quit!"

He grabbed Ginger by the shoulders. "Quick, blow the whistle! We gotta get out of here!"

Ginger shoved him off. "We just got here, you dimwit."

"Uh, guys?" I said. *"Guys!"*

Ginger and Manuel stopped arguing, and everyone looked down at the red cap.

His face was bright red, and he was huffing and puffing like he was going to explode.

"You said that things like anger get them riled up?" whispered Asma.

"Oh, shoot," moaned Ginger.

Then it happened. The red cap multiplied.

There was a "pop!" and suddenly a second red cap appeared out of thin air. Then another.

Another "pop!" and one landed in Asma's hair. "Gross! Get it off! There's no telling where it's been!" she screamed.

It sounded like a popcorn popper in there, but instead of kernels flying around, the air was filled with red caps. They went for the backpacks and began grabbing whatever they could find. Food, socks. One of them stuck a mini box of Corn Flakes over its head.

"Hey!" shouted Ginger. "That's my breakfast!" She charged after the little creature, but it ducked under a broken table, bumped into the wall (remember, it had a box of cereal over its head), and scurried out of reach.

Ginger's face was getting redder by the minute as she tried, and failed, to catch the little monsters.

Another snatched Manuel's video game out of his hand and began maniacally pushing random buttons.

Asma ran for the door, but it was blocked by a whole group of red caps squirting hand sanitizer at anyone who came too close.

We grabbed the butterfly nets and mason jars and tried to catch them, but the creatures were too fast. And when we did manage to snag one, it would go "pop!" and produce three more.

"Wait!" I shouted, trying desperately to get my friends' attention. "We have to calm down, everyone! We're just making it worse."

But then something tripped me as I was going by. I fell face-first onto the dusty floor, and suddenly I was covered in a swarm of little red-capped beasties. They pinched, tickled, and blew raspberries at me until I managed to swat them away.

When I was finally able to stand, my boots were gone.

This was a disaster. The door was blocked and soon we'd be up to our knees in red caps. "Ginger!" I yelled. "Blow the stupid whistle!"

Ginger was busy playing whack-a-mole with a frying pan and two red caps.

"GINGER!" Asma, Manuel, and I all shouted at once.

"Fine!" She dropped the pan and put the whistle to her lips. She blew, and a clear, high-pitched whistle rang out into the night.

Everyone froze, even the red caps.

She blew it again, but nothing happened.

"Where's Spitzer?" asked Asma.

I shooed a group of red caps away from a chair and climbed on it to look out the nearest window. There was the bus, but no Spitzer. He was nowhere in sight.

There was no one to come to the rescue.

And with a shout of triumph, the red caps resumed their super annoying frenzy.

"Wheeeeeeeeeeee!" they cried.

We were done for.

8

A BIG FISH IN A SMALL POND

So that's how I ended up bootless in a Scottish lighthouse that was swarming with little red-capped beasties.

And I still hadn't seen a real live haggis.

But the story doesn't end there. In fact, the real excitement was about to start. Because just when I thought things couldn't get scarier and the red caps had reached their height of beastiness, the lighthouse started to shake.

It began as a low rumble that could barely be heard over the red caps' party, but then it grew into a roar. Dust fell from the rafters, and a few red caps did, too, as the whole lighthouse trembled. Everyone, even the red caps, stood stock-still as an enormous shadow passed by the windows, blocking out the moon.

Something was outside the

lighthouse, and that something was huge.

Then we heard the loud crash of metal twisting and glass breaking, followed by the sound of something big splashing around in the water.

Hey, here's something the book didn't mention about red caps—they're also little cowards. Because one minute they were there and the next, gone. They scurried into hiding so fast they left my boots behind.

As for Troop D, we waited until all was quiet. Then we crept outside.

Everything was a complete mess. Something had crushed the bus like a tin can, and the ground all around was flattened, like something enormous had dragged itself across it. And just like at the wind farm, the trail led back to the misty lake.

"Uh, guys?" said Asma. "Did Nessie just wreck our bus?"

It sure looked like it. What else coming out of that lake could have done so much damage? It was an awful possibility to think about.

After all these years of peacefully avoiding humans, why would Nessie start smashing up the shore now?

"Wh-what? What happened to our bus?" a voice sputtered from behind us.

We turned to see Spitzer standing there, mouth open in shock. He had his golf clubs slung over one shoulder and a stuffed lake monster under his arm.

"I leave you alone for one hour and look at this!" he said. "What did you do?"

"*We* didn't do anything," snapped Ginger. "Other than get our behinds whooped by red caps while our *chaperone* played Putt-Putt golf!"

Spitzer's sneer cracked, and suddenly he looked worried. "I . . . I only played a few rounds. I just needed to get the trophy." He held up the stuffed lake monster.

Ginger slapped her forehead. "That's not a trophy, it's a toy!"

"Says someone who knows nothing about the art of miniature golf!" said Spitzer as he hugged his toy closer to him.

I had had enough.

"Can we *please* stop arguing about golf?" I shouted. As my voice echoed along the shore, I suddenly heard the

chitter of little voices drifting from the lighthouse.

"Better keep your voice down," warned Asma.

I sighed. "Asma's right. Let's all take a deep breath and calm down, because it's no use arguing about what's already happened. I think our bigger worry is Nessie." I pointed to those weird, slithery tracks leading to the lake. "If she did this to our bus, there's no telling what else she might do."

But Spitzer, surprisingly, disagreed. "She wouldn't do this. Not in a million years."

"You have another explanation?" asked Manuel. "Our bus didn't implode by itself."

"I don't know," said Spitzer. "But if you scouts failed Walter's red cap test as spectacularly as it appears, we may never find out."

"Test?" I said. "What do you mean?"

Spitzer laughed bitterly. "You haven't figured it out yet? This trip to Scotland is a ritual for the Strange Scouts, and meeting Nessie is only the final part. First you gotta prove you can work as a team, keep your cool, and overcome your fear. If you don't, you'll remain *junior* scouts forever."

So the lighthouse was a *test*? That felt super unfair. Pop quizzes are bad enough, but at least you know you're taking a pop quiz when it starts. "You could have told us."

"What more did you need to know?"

asked Spitzer. "Being a scout isn't about doing the right thing when you're expected to—it's about doing the right thing all the time."

"Hey, it wasn't a total failure," said Manuel. He held up a glass mason jar. "I caught one of them."

Inside the mason jar was a single red cap, sound asleep. The little guy had tuckered himself out. If you listened closely, you could even hear his tiny snores.

"What are you doing!" whispered Spitzer. "Aren't you all in enough trouble?"

Manuel blushed. "Okay, I'll let him loose." He started to unscrew the lid.

But Spitzer frantically shook his head. "No! Not here! Take that thing back inside."

"I'm not going back in there," said Manuel. "You do it."

Spitzer paled. He looked like he'd rather eat an entire haggis than step one foot inside that lighthouse. "Fine," he sighed. "Just put it away. We'll figure out what to do with it later."

With a shrug, Manuel stowed the jarred red cap safely inside his backpack.

But Ginger wasn't about to let Spitzer off that easily. "We're not the

only ones in trouble. You were supposed
to be watching us!"

"None of that matters," said Asma.
"Because I don't think this"—she
pointed to the ruined bus—"was part
of the test, was it?"

"No," confirmed Spitzer. "There's
something fishy going on."

"Asma's right." Jeez, was that
the second time I'd said that in five
minutes? "We may stay junior scouts
forever, but right now I think we need
to find whatever did that to our bus."

"And if it is Nessie?" asked Manuel,
worried.

"Well, let's hope the handbook has
something useful in it about dealing
with out-of-control lake monsters."

At the mention of the handbook,
Spitzer gave me a look. "Shouldn't we

wait for Walter?" he asked. "He said he'd be back at dawn."

"That's like eight hours away," I said. "If Nessie really is on a rampage, people could be in danger. We need to protect them."

Asma, Ginger, and even Manuel nodded. "That's what Strange Scouts do," said Asma. Then she recited the Strange Scouts Oath, word for word:

**On my honor I will do my best:
To honor Mother Nature and all her creations, especially the monstrous ones, to help my fellow citizens of the world, to preserve oddity and strangeness in all its glory, especially my own, because uniqueness is never weakness.**

Darn, she was right again! Even

Spitzer gave in. "Fine. But I'm still the adult around here, so when we get out there, you kids do what I say. Promise?"

We promised. Of course, each one of us had our fingers crossed behind our backs, but hey, if it made Spitzer feel better, then why not?

"Okay, so now that we all agree that we're honorable and honest scouts doing the right thing, I only have one question," I said. "Anyone know where we can steal a boat?"

PADDLE YOUR OWN CANOE

In the end, we didn't actually have to steal a boat, since Spitzer just rented one instead. Adventures are a lot easier when you're a grown-up with your own wallet and credit cards and stuff.

Still, it took us a few hours to find

a boat place that would rent to us at night and ignore the constable's order to keep tourists off the lake. But I think the kind old lady who ran the boat shop thought our scout uniforms made us look important. Like we were FBI agents in shorts and neckerchiefs.

Unfortunately, Spitzer had already blown most of his money on mini-golf, so all we could afford was a small

rowboat with a tiny outboard motor. I was just glad it had a motor at all, because did I mention that Loch Ness is twenty-three miles long? You try rowing that far. You can tell me how it went after your arms fall off.

Loch Ness was covered in a heavy fog that night, and our flashlights barely helped. We decided to follow the shoreline so we wouldn't get lost, but the mist was so thick that it was easy to lose sight of land.

"What exactly are we looking for?" asked Manuel after about half an hour of floating aimlessly.

"The Loch Ness Monster, duh!" said Ginger.

"I know that!" he said. "I meant are we looking for any special signs, like

something that would tell us we're on the right track?"

"Good question," said Asma. "It's probably time to check the handbook, right, Ben?"

"Yeah, you're right." Darn it, I did it *again*!

As I slipped it out of my backpack, I caught Spitzer eyeing his old handbook, but he didn't say anything. He'd made it very clear back at Camp Spirit that he wanted nothing to do with it anymore. "Shine your flashlight over here," I said to Manuel.

With Manuel's help, I found the page titled "Nessie, the Loch Ness Monster" and began reading. "Says here that Nessie stays away from humans whenever possible, and only appears to a very fortunate few."

"Walter already told us all that," complained Ginger.

"Hold on," I said. "There's more. 'While being rather large, Nessie is surprisingly quiet, having learned to swim and even to walk on land with almost total stealth.'"

"That doesn't sound like the thing that smashed our bus," said Asma. "I could barely think because of all the noise."

"Hmm," said Manuel. "Could there be a second Loch Ness Monster? Like an evil twin Nessie?"

No one answered right away because we were all thinking about how vulnerable we were out there on the lake at night, in a tiny boat.

"Give me your light again, Manuel," I said. "There's a bunch of handwritten notes here. Maybe they can tell us some—"

Without warning, Spitzer reached over and slammed the book shut, nearly catching my fingers.

"That's enough reading!" he said. "Put the book away. We're heading back to shore. This was a bad idea."

I didn't know what had gotten into Spitzer, but odds were he'd written those notes as a kid and for some reason didn't want to revisit them.

Of course, this only made me want to read them more. And *out loud*. To everyone. But seeing as I didn't want to swim back to shore, I obediently put the book back in my pack.

"Where is shore, exactly?" asked Asma.

"We can't navigate by starlight with

all this fog," said Spitzer. "But I think
I see something up ahead. It's hard to
tell in the dark, but it might be a dock."

I peered into the mist. He was right.
By the light of our flashlights, it did
look like there was a shape, low and
close to the water.

And coming our way.

"It's moving!" I whispered.

"Don't be silly," said Spitzer. "We're moving."

But Asma pointed. "I think Ben's right!"

Finally!

"Brace yourselves!" I cried. "It's coming straight for us!"

A DrOp In THE OcEaN

O kay, maybe my shouting "Brace yourselves!" was a little dramatic, but all that talk of an evil Loch Ness Monster really had me on edge.

The truth is, while the mysterious shape in the water was definitely heading our way, it was doing so slowly.

Very slowly. Like about as fast as an old man rowing a boat would go.

"Ahoy!" called a familiar voice.

Like I said earlier, you'd have to be crazy to try to row across Loch Ness.

Unless you were Walter.

The old Scout Master was rowing with gusto, I'll give him that. He was

in an even smaller boat than ours, and there was no motor.

"Walter, what are you doing?" sighed Spitzer.

"I'm looking for Nessie!" huffed Walter. "What are you doing? You all are supposed to be back at the lighthouse."

"Nessie smashed our bus!" said Ginger. She skipped over the part where we totally failed with the red caps, but, you know, priorities!

"We didn't actually see what did it," I added. "But whatever it was, it came from the lake."

Walter scratched his beard. "Hmm. None of this sounds like Nessie. What could have riled the old girl up so?"

"I remembered the Strange Scouts

Oath and recited it by heart," said Asma. "I thought if we could help, it was our duty to do so."

"Oh, brother," muttered Manuel.

"Can't say I'm happy with you all putting yourselves in danger," said Walter. "But I admire your spunk!"

"Oh, brother," muttered Spitzer.

Walter wiped the fog from his glasses. "Little while back, I caught a glimpse of something in the fog that *might* be Nessie, but it's so hard to tell in all this dang mist."

"What'd it look like?" I asked. "Roughly."

"Well, let's see, roughly it looked . . ." He put his glasses back on. "Like that!"

Suddenly something came out of the fog. It was still hard to make out details, but we saw a long neck, taller than a house, attached to a wide snout. It was the Loch Ness Monster, and it was coming right at us!

"Brace yourselves!" I cried. "For real!"

WhEn It RaINs, It PoUrS

This time when I shouted "Brace yourselves!" I meant it, because Nessie was coming straight for us—fast. She must've been angry about something, as that rumbling roar was louder than ever.

Spitzer threw the motor into high

gear, and we started speeding out of there, but poor Walter didn't have a hope of rowing fast enough to avoid getting capsized by the lake monster.

"We gotta save Walter!" I yelled.

Ginger, who'd been digging around in the bottom of the boat, found a life preserver attached to a rope. On the count of three, we threw it as hard as we could. Walter grabbed the life preserver and jumped just in the nick of time, right as his boat was crushed to splinters by the passing monster.

It took the combined strength of all of Troop D to haul old Walter to safety. For a skinny guy, he weighed a ton!

Once we were clear of the monster's wake, Spitzer slowed down as Nessie

disappeared once more into the fog.

Walter coughed up about a gallon of lake water at our feet.

"Eww," said Asma.

"I . . . I can't believe Nessie would do something like that," said Spitzer. It was hard to tell in the dark, but he looked like he actually had tears in his eyes.

Boy, people sure can surprise you.

"She wouldn't," said Walter, still gasping for breath. "This isn't right."

"Hey." Manuel sniffed the air. "Anyone smell something weird?"

Asma held her nose. "Yeah, it's really strong."

One by one, we all looked at Walter.

"Jehoshaphat!" the old man exclaimed. "It's me! I'm covered in motor oil!"

Ginger shined the flashlight on Walter. A black sheen covered his hair and clothes.

"Where'd that come from?" she asked.

"Must've been in the water when Walter fell in," I said. "Gimme your light again, Manuel."

I shined the flashlight at the water behind us. Sure enough, there was a trail of oil floating along the water. It followed the exact same path Nessie had just taken, toward shore.

"Since when do lake monsters leak motor oil?" asked Manuel.

"Since never," said Walter. "Spitzer, turn this boat around and follow that oil trail!"

For once, Spitzer didn't argue.

In fact, he followed Walter's orders without hesitation. "Aye, aye, Captain!" And together, Troop D sped off into the night! Into danger!

(Cue the awesome action-movie music, okay?)

SLIPPERY WHEN WET

T though it was still foggy, the mist thinned out a bit as we got closer to shore. We'd followed the oil

slick into a cove hidden by tall cliffs on either side. A long wooden dock stretched out into the lake from a sandy beach. A stairway led to a large lake house and garage.

"Look!" exclaimed Ginger. "It's Nessie!"

Tied up to the dock was a massive lake monster.

"What's she doing?" whispered Manuel. "She's just floating there. She's not even moving."

"Hmm," said Walter. "Let's get a

little closer, but quietly!"

Spitzer cut the motor, and we used the oars to paddle the rest of the way.

"Shine your flashlights there." We aimed our lights up at the monster and finally saw the truth close-up. This "Nessie" was actually sitting in a small ferry, and the lake monster's head and neck were cold, unmoving plastic.

"Look!" I whispered. "She's on treads." The monster's lower half ended in massive treads and metal machinery. A long rubber tarp was attached to the back. "That's what destroyed that wind farm and smashed our bus. It's a bulldozer dressed up like a monster!"

"I don't get it," said Manuel. "Why

is someone driving that crazy thing around?"

"Because someone wants to blame all this destruction on Nessie," I said. "Think about it—the ferry pulls up to shore, and the bulldozer drives up the beach and smashes whatever's in its path. If anyone catches a glimpse, they just see the monster's head in the mist. And it drags that big rubber tarp behind it to erase the tread tracks in the sand."

"And I think we've all seen that plastic lake monster before," said Asma. "Or its twin."

"Yeah," said Ginger. "Right, Spitzer?"

The Scout Master looked crushed, but he nodded. "There's one just like it at MacGregor's Classic Golf Green. If you get a hole in one, you get your very own stuffed Nessie."

Manuel looked over at Walter, who'd been quiet. "Walter, what are we going to do?"

The old man tugged at his beard for a moment. "This is a matter for local authorities now. It ain't the real Nessie doing these crimes, so that means we need to get the constable involved. Troop D, I want you to sneak ashore and keep an eye on that house. If MacGregor is in there, he might try something again tonight. You keep watch but do not, I repeat, do *not* try to engage him in any way. Got it?"

We nodded. "Where are you and Spitzer going?" I asked.

"We gotta convince the constable

that a mini-golf millionaire is destroying lakeshore property with a bulldozer dressed up like a monster. I'd say we've got a better chance at that than a bunch of kids do."

We rowed the boat close to the beach, and Manuel, Asma, Ginger, and I waded to shore through the cold water.

"We'll be back with the constable as soon as we can," said Walter. "Remember, watch but do not go anywhere near MacGregor! Got it?"

"Got it," we said, all together.

"Promise?"

"Scout's honor," we answered, and then Spitzer and Walter turned on the boat's motor and disappeared into the mist.

And before you ask, yes, we totally had our fingers crossed behind our backs. Again. But I mean, what kind of story would this be if we always followed the rules?

HoOk, LiNE, AnD SinKEr

Walter and Spitzer weren't gone five minutes before MacGregor stepped out of the lake house. He stood there for a while, smoking a smelly cigar, then started down the stairs toward the dock.

"Guys," I whispered. "What if MacGregor gets into that ferry and

takes off with the fake Nessie?"

"So?" said Asma. "We've seen him. We'll just tell the constable what happened when he gets here."

"And you think he'll believe the word of a bunch of kids over one of the town's richest men? That fake monster is the only real evidence that he ran over that wind farm and ruined our bus. If he hides it, there's no case."

"Oh, wow," said Manuel. "Ben's right." Thank you.

"So what do we do?" asked Ginger. "We can't just *ask* him to wait around for the cops!"

She was right. MacGregor had already reached the dock and was starting to untie the ferry. Either he was off to do more damage, or he was going to get rid of the evidence.

"We need a plan and we need one fast!" warned Asma.

"I'm thinking, I'm thinking!" I said. "It's not like these things just pop into your head. . . . Wait, that's it!"

It was brilliant. And crazy. Okay, mostly crazy, but it was all I could think of at the time. I whispered my idea to Troop D, and after they'd finished telling me I was out of my mind, Manuel said, "You know, it just might work!"

Teamwork was the key. If we could get close enough, Manuel and I were pretty sure we could disable MacGregor's bulldozing monster, but we needed a distraction. That's where Ginger and Asma came in.

MacGregor had just hopped aboard the ferry when he saw flashlights shining up at his lake house. We knew he saw them because the girls purposely made enough noise to wake the dead.

See, the idea was to make MacGregor think someone was snooping around his house so he'd go see who it was. Ginger and Asma would turn off the flashlights and hightail it out of there. While MacGregor searched for the intruders in vain, Manuel and I would sneak up to the dock under cover of darkness and sabotage his ferry. There would be no way for MacGregor to escape before the constable arrived.

Brilliant, right? Well, we ran into a few problems.

In their attempt to distract MacGregor, Asma and Ginger tripped his home security system. An alarm started to wail and floodlights shined out everywhere.

Manuel and I were about halfway across the beach when suddenly it was as bright as day. So yeah, that was the first problem.

The second was that MacGregor was totally psychotic. Who knew?

"You!" cried MacGregor. "Why, I'll

teach you to trespass on my property!"

He hopped into the cab of his bulldozer monster and literally cackled as the engine roared to life. This plastic lake monster didn't just breathe smoke—it breathed fire!

And it was coming for us.

Manuel and I were helpless. There was nowhere to hide on the beach, and I doubted we could outrun that thing in the sand. But luckily, our troop mates didn't abandon us.

Asma and Ginger began pelting MacGregor with rocks, clumps of mud—whatever they could find. The evil businessman roared almost as loud as his engine as he turned the bulldozer to face them.

"No one throws mud at Martin Mac— OOF!" Ginger had found MacGregor's trash cans and had just beaned him in the face with a rotten tomato. Attagirl!

She'd gotten his attention, all right.

The bulldozer started climbing the hill toward the house. Toward Ginger and Asma.

I started to run up the hill after him. "C'mon! Plan B!"

"What's plan B?" asked Manuel as he struggled to keep up.

"Give me your backpack!"

"Why?"

"Just do it!"

"Okay!" He tossed it to me. "Careful, though, my games are in there, man!"

I yanked open the pack and shoved my hand inside. I wasn't looking for video games.

With all the commotion and panicking, the red cap was already looking pretty upset. He shook his fist at me as he bounced around inside the jar. He was starting to turn beet red.

Good.

We reached the bulldozer just as it was bearing down on Asma and Ginger, who'd armed themselves with an assortment of rotten vegetables. With Manuel's help, I pried the lid off the jar and, with a heave, tossed the red cap at the machine monster.

POP! Pop pop pop-pop-pop-pop-pop-pop!

It took about three seconds for the bulldozer to become overrun by red caps. They flipped switches and pushed buttons, bringing the machine to a sudden halt.

MacGregor cried out as one of them yanked the toupee off his head and another snapped his suspenders.

Still screaming, he bolted from

the bulldozer and made for the ferry,
batting away red caps as he ran.

"He's getting away," said Manuel,
but we were too far away to stop him.

And then a strange thing happened.
An enormous shadow appeared in the
foggy lake. It was headed for the dock,
picking up speed, but then it veered off
at the last second, causing a massive
wave to rise up out of the lake and
smash into the dock. When the water

cleared, the ferry had capsized and
was sinking fast.

Meanwhile, the wave had lifted
MacGregor and deposited him halfway
up the beach. He was soaking wet,
shaking, and as pale as chalk. He looked
like he'd just seen a ghost.

Or a monster.

A WHALE OF A TIME

As the constable took MacGregor away in handcuffs, the businessman confessed to everything. He also kept babbling on and on about how the Loch Ness Monster had destroyed his ferry. Of course, no one believed him except us, but who would trust the word of a bunch of kids, anyway?

It turned out it was all about the wind farms. MacGregor thought the wind farms looked "tacky" and might drive away customers—and this coming from a guy who owned a Putt-Putt golf course. The wind farms were a safe and clean source of energy, but all he cared about was his business. So he devised a plan to wreck the farms and blame it on the Loch Ness Monster.

What a weirdo.

As for Troop D, we gathered our things and met back at the lighthouse to prepare for the trip home. Thankfully, the red caps seemed to have quieted down. Ginger said that before we left MacGregor's place, she caught a glimpse of a red hat in one of the house's windows, so I don't think anyone will be moving in there anytime soon.

It was sunrise, and as we waited for a cab to take us back to the airport, Walter assembled us at the shore. He lined us up with our backs to the water and started to lecture us.

We all knew what was coming— we'd failed the red cap test. We were going to remain junior scouts.

"Scouts," he said. "Never in all my years as a Scout Master has a troop failed the red cap test so spectacularly. . . ."

I couldn't look Walter in the eye, so I stared at my shoes instead.

"And yet, never has a troop showed such bravery and teamwork when it really counted."

Huh?

"Ben Beederman, step forward. You have earned the following badges: Teamwork, Good Deeds, and Creative Red Cap Handling. Congratulations, Strange Scout, First Class!"

First Class! Man, that just sounds cool, doesn't it?

"What about my troop mates?" I asked. "They were just as—"

But Walter chuckled. "Hold your horses. I was getting to them."

One by one, he pinned badges on Manuel, Ginger, and Asma. The four of us glowed with pride.

"Uh, Walter," said Ginger. "I hate to say it, but there's one more person who really did help."

"Yeah," said Manuel, "Spitzer's a pain, but he's sorta one of us. Sorta."

Walter grinned. "Turn around."

We looked back at the lake. Spitzer was down by the beach, and as the sun broke over the calm water, the mist parted for just a moment.

There was Nessie. She wasn't a fierce beast like the plastic phony MacGregor had mocked up—she was beautiful. Her scales shimmered silver in the morning sun.

As we watched her slowly swim to shore, Spitzer held up his hand, and Nessie bowed her head. Spitzer petted her gently as he whispered something too softly for us to hear.

I cracked open the scout handbook

to the chapter on Nessie. There, written in the margins in Spitzer's very own handwriting, was the following, the words he didn't want us to read:

P.S. Just met Nessie for the first time today, and this handbook doesn't have it even half right about her. She's amazing, and I think I might have finally found a new best friend. I hope I can come back someday.

Walter leaned in close to us and said, "Long ago, I introduced a shy, lonely boy named William Spitzer to Nessie, and she changed his life, made him see the world in a whole new light—for a while, at least. And once a Strange Scout, always a Strange Scout. No matter how hard he might protest. Remember this moment, kids."

No one really talked much on the ride to the airport. I guess we were all kind of letting it sink in. Spitzer was in a daze most of the way, but by the time we got out of the cab, he was back to barking orders at us to straighten up and pay attention.

Oh, well. Quiet Spitzer was good while it lasted.

After a bit of arguing, Walter

finally agreed to let us fly a commercial airline back home and put the *Green Goose* in retirement, at least until she could be spruced up. By the time we took our seats on the plane, our stomachs were growling so loudly that people were starting to give us looks.

A smiling flight attendant came by and offered me a menu. "Would you like to purchase an entrée for the flight?" she asked.

I glanced back at Walter to make sure it was okay. (I was used to little baggies of peanuts and that's all.) But Walter nodded and said, "Why not? Go ahead and order something for the troop, Ben. Surprise us."

While the attendant waited for my order, I scanned the menu.

And there it was. A glorious ending to an unforgettable adventure.

"We'll have the haggis," I said.

MATTHEW CODY is the acclaimed author of several popular children's books, including the award-winning Supers of Noble's Green trilogy: *Powerless*, *Super*, and *Villainous*. He lives in New York City with his wife and son.

STEVE LAMBE is an Emmy Award–winning animator for such TV shows as *The Fairly OddParents*, *Teen Titans Go!*, and *The Mighty B!* He has also illustrated several Golden Books. He lives in Ontario, Canada, with his wife and son.

Also in the series:

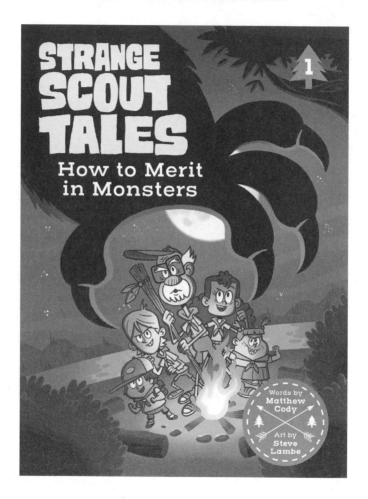

AVAILABLE NOW!